Megabat was looking forward to Christmas morning: opening presents, playing toys, eating smooshfruit and watching *Star Wars*. But then Daniel opened his last, most special present.

Daniel thinks this might be the best Christmas gift yet: a beautiful cat named Priscilla! He's always wanted a pet.

Megabat is not sure he likes this cat. She tastes most hairy.

Daniel loves his new cat! She's fun to play with, and she's so soft and fluffy.

Megabat is not soft OR fluffy. He's not purebred and he doesn't have a big, beautiful swishy tail. What if Daniel loves Priscilla more than Megabat? This is truly a disturbance in the Force. Megabat and Birdgirl must find a way to get rid of this trubble cat once and for all!

Paperback edition published by Tundra Books, 2020

Text copyright © 2019 by Anna Humphrey
Illustrations copyright © 2019 by Kass Reich

Tundra Books, an imprint of Penguin Random House Canada Young Readers,
a Penguin Random House Company

Library and Archives Canada Cataloguing in Publication

Title: Megabat and Fancy Cat / Anna Humphrey ; illustrated by Kass Reich.
Names: Humphrey, Anna, author. | Reich, Kass, illustrator.
Series: Humphrey, Anna. Megabat (Series)
Description: Series statement: Megabat
Identifiers: Canadiana 20190201657 | ISBN 9780735267114 (softcover)
Classification: LCC PS8615.U457 M45 2020 | DDC jC813/.6—dc23

Published simultaneously in the United States of America by Tundra Books of
Northern New York, an imprint of Penguin Random House Canada Young Readers,
a Penguin Random House Company

Library of Congress Control Number: 2018937030

Edited by Samantha Swenson
Designed by Andrew Roberts and John Martz
The artwork in this book was rendered in graphite.
The text was set in Caslon 540 LT Std.

Printed and bound in the United States of America

www.penguinrandomhouse.ca

1   2   3   4   5   24   23   22   21   20

Penguin
Random House
tundra   TUNDRA BOOKS

ANNA HUMPHREY   illustrated by
KASS REICH

MEGA BAT

AND
FANCY CAT

tundra

For Naomi, Ida and Margot:
the fierce & fancy
Tanentzapf girls

THE SURPRISE

The day the cat arrived started out special but ended up spoiled.

It was Christmas morning, and Megabat was dreaming. He was deep in the jungles of Borneo, about to feast on fruit so fresh it was still on the vine. He could smell a heavenly aroma.

"Mmmmmmm," the tiny fruit bat said. He began to rock back and forth.

"Mellllons," he drooled.

"Guess again," he heard his friend Daniel say—as if from a great distance.

"Lemmmmons."

"Not quite." The dream was drifting away. Daniel sounded closer now.

The bat squinted one eye open. He was in the backyard shed, hanging upside down from the beam where he always slept. Beneath his snout, his friend was holding a plump, juicy mandarin orange! Quick as a flash, Megabat grabbed it in his wingtips. "Gots it!" he cried triumphantly, and plunged his snout in.

Daniel laughed. "Good morning. And happy holidays."

"Yes, yes," Megabat said between slurps of juice. "Joyous day of the dead tree."

It was Megabat's first Christmas in Canada. Not so long ago, he'd lived on a papaya farm in Borneo with other fruit bats who'd never heard of Christmas either. The whole thing was strange to him.

Besides the baffling tradition of dragging a dead tree into the house, it was the idea of Santa that had him most confused.

"The man is too fatish and oldish to be climbing stairs?" Megabat had asked when Daniel showed him a picture of Santa sliding down the chimney.

"Well, no. I mean, Santa's old… with a big, round belly… but that's not why he comes down the chimney. I guess it's because he doesn't have keys to the houses."

Megabat gasped. "Santa is being a rotten robber!" He tapped one talon on the picture, which showed a row of stockings hung along a mantel. "His is having large feets." Megabat studied Santa's big black boots. "Therefores, his comes for stealing the giant socks."

"He doesn't *take* the socks," Daniel had explained with a smile. "He brings presents and puts them inside. The big socks are called stockings."

At that, the bat's eyes lit up. Because

even though Megabat was puzzled by Christmas, he understood presents. In fact, he was a huge fan.

"Presents for Megabat?" he'd said.

Daniel had promised there would be... and now the big day had finally arrived.

Daniel produced a rectangle-shaped package from behind his back. It had a shiny silver bow on top.

Megabat flapped his wings in excitement. "Santa has filled the sock-things!"

"*Stockings*," Daniel corrected. He took a bag from his coat pocket and set it on the beam. "And I bet he brought us lots of presents. But these ones are from me."

Megabat examined the tag on the bag. "Birdgirl!" he called down to his beloved, a pretty-pretty pigeon who was still asleep in her nest underneath his beam. She lifted her snowy white head and looked up at him groggily. "There's being a present for you." Over the last few weeks, Daniel and his friend Talia had been teaching Megabat and Birdgirl to read. They were getting better every day. Megabat had recognized the B-I-R-D *birrrrd* sound on the tag straight away.

"Coo-woo!" The pigeon bobbed her head when she saw that the bag was filled with sunflower seeds.

It really was a thoughtful gift.

"The puffer rats will not be getting *those*, Birdgirl," Megabat said with a satisfied smile.

Ever since the autumn, the no-good puffer rats that lurked in Daniel's yard had been stealing the birdseed Daniel's mother set out each morning. She used to put it in the old bird feeder in the tree, but now that the feeder had started to come loose and tilt to one side, she just threw the seeds onto the lawn instead. And because the rats were frisky *and* ferocious, poor Birdgirl rarely got her fair share.

"They're actually called squirrels," Daniel reminded him. But Megabat had seen enough rotten rats to recognize one when he saw it—even if these ones *did* have strange puffy tails.

"And this"—Daniel put the big present down—"is for you, Megabat."

"*Merr-why Ch-rist-mass*, Megabat," he read off the tag. The bat plucked the bow off and stuck it firmly to the top of his head. Then he tore into the paper, scattering bits everywhere.

"Ooooooooh!" he said. It was a six-pack of juice boxes. Apple-boysenberry. His favorite.

"Come on. Christmas isn't over yet." Daniel held out his hand for Megabat to perch on. "Mom and Dad are making pancakes, and then it'll be time for more presents."

Megabat gasped. "Waiting! Waiting!" He took off toward the back of the shed where Daniel's parents kept the recycling box. He could hardly believe he'd forgotten to wrap the present he'd made for his very best friend, but thankfully there was still time. He covered the gift

in crumpled newspaper, then took the
big silver bow Daniel had just given him
and stuck it on top.

"Present!" he declared moments later,
dropping his creation on Daniel's head.
Daniel fumbled, trying to catch it, then
bent down to pick it up.

"Is yours *loving* it?" Megabat asked, flapping his wings eagerly as Daniel unwrapped the gift.

"Umm… sure?" Daniel examined the thing.

The present was made of a toilet paper roll with a tinfoil ball shoved into one end.

"Is R2-D2!" Megabat said. "Looking!"

Daniel's face lit up. Watching Star Wars movies was one of their favorite things to do—and the droid named R2-D2 was the character they liked most.

"Oh yeah!" he said. "Thanks, Megabat."

The two friends left Birdgirl to her

seeds and went inside. "Shhhh," Daniel said, reminding Megabat to keep quiet and out of sight. He slipped the bat into his bathrobe pocket. Daniel's mother was terrified of bats. If she ever found out there was one in the house, she'd scream.

"There you are!" Daniel's mom walked past with a plate of pancakes and ruffled his hair. "Would you grab the maple syrup?"

As they sat down to breakfast, Megabat could see the stacks of brightly wrapped presents in the living room. Eating took forever, but finally it was time to open gifts.

There was Lego and a new video game, art supplies, a hat with earflaps

and even a paint-your-own model steam engine that would really drive around a track. It was just the right size for Megabat to sit in!

Megabat gasped quietly inside Daniel's pocket as each new present was revealed. All in all, it was a great haul, but then…

"Hang on," Daniel's mom announced. "There's one more surprise." Daniel's parents shared a secret smile before his mom waded through the ripped-up wrapping paper and disappeared upstairs.

PRISCILLA

A minute later Daniel's mother was back, carrying a large, beige plastic box with holes in it. It wasn't wrapped in shiny paper. It didn't even have a bow. If it was a present, it looked like a boring one to Megabat.

"This…" she said grandly, "is much more than just a gift. It's a brand-new family member. Daniel, I'd like you to meet Priscilla: our very own cat!" Daniel's mom set the box down gently.

Daniel dropped to his knees on the carpet. "No way!"

"Now that we're living in a bigger house," his dad started, "your mother thought—"

"It was a good time to get a pet," his mom finished. "And then, when Mrs. Cormier down the street told me she'd developed allergies to her cat, Priscilla, well… it just seemed like a perfect solution that she come live with us instead! Isn't she gorgeous?"

The cat was huddled at the back of the carrier. When Daniel leaned forward, Megabat peeked out of his pocket. All he could see were two shining eyes staring back at him—that is, until Daniel's dad reached down and opened the cage door.

The first things to emerge were the whiskers. They were long and silky— and above them was a small brown nose twitching madly.

"That's it, little kitty," Daniel's mom cooed. "Don't be scared."

The cat stuck her head out and looked both ways. Her eyes were the color of a clear sky; her fur yellowy white, like vanilla ice cream. And she had warm chocolate patches on her face and ears.

"I'll get her some kibble," Daniel's mom said.

"And I'll set up the litter box," Daniel's dad said. "We'll let you two get acquainted."

Once the coast was clear, Megabat crawled onto Daniel's shoulder to get a better look. Now that the cat had come all the way out, he could see that she looked bunny-rabbit soft. Her tail was as fluffy as the feather duster Daniel's dad used on the shelves.

"She's the prettiest cat ever!" Daniel said.

Megabat had seen cats before. They often walked across the top of the fence in the backyard. But he'd never seen one so clean, so silky or so close-up.

"Oooooh!" Megabat teetered from side to side. "So niiiiice!" She really was wonderful. And when Megabat liked something—like, really, really liked it...

SLUUUUURP!

His super-long tongue flew toward the cat like a fishing line. He'd only meant to lick the top of the cat's head, but she moved, so instead his tongue caught her across the face with a slobbery slap.

RE-OOOOOOWWWW!

The cat leapt onto the coffee table and launched herself at the Christmas tree. For a second, she clung to the branches in the middle while a few ornaments clattered to the floor—and it looked like things might turn out mostly okay—but then the tree started to tilt, the cat began paddling at the air with her back feet, and they both went down with a glittery, howling crash.

"What happened?!" Daniel's mom ran in from the kitchen just in time to see the cat dash around the toppled tree, leap over a pile of smashed ornaments and disappear under the couch, trailing a sparkly strand of garland from her tail.

Megabat dropped from Daniel's shoulder into his bathrobe pocket before he could be spotted.

"She tried to climb the tree," Daniel said, leaving out the part about how the cat had been startled by the sudden lick of a talking fruit bat.

"Here we go," said Daniel's dad, who had rushed in as well. "Didn't I warn you that getting a cat would be trouble?"

"She hasn't even been here an hour," Daniel's mother said reasonably. "The poor thing must be terrified. She'll settle in."

After that, Daniel was told to go wait in the kitchen while his parents cleaned up the broken glass ornaments.

"Megabat!" Daniel scolded, as soon as they were safely out of earshot of his parents. "Don't ever do that again!"

Megabat huffed. After all, it was *the cat* who'd knocked over the tree. He'd only just licked her hello.

"Cats don't like being licked," Daniel explained.

"That's being not true!" Megabat argued. He'd seen many cats lie in the sun licking themselves. "Licking is a cat's very favorite!" Although, now that he knew how hairy a cat tasted, he couldn't understand why. He stuck out his tongue and scraped at it with his wingtips to get the fur off.

"Here," Daniel said, taking a cold pancake off a stack of leftovers. "Why don't you bring this back to the shed and give it to Birdgirl?"

"But… what's about playing toys?" Megabat wailed.

After breakfast, there was supposed

to be time to play with the new toys—
like the steam engine that Megabat
could sit inside—then lunchtime, board
games and hot apple cider.

In response, Daniel held the back
door open. "You can come back
tomorrow, okay? After Priscilla's had
some time to get settled. We'll play
then."

Megabat draped the cold pancake over
his shoulders and made big, sad eyes at
his friend, but Daniel didn't seem to
notice. He was already looking back
toward the living room, where the cat
was still hiding.

A FANCY SPLAT

All afternoon and well into the evening, Megabat fumed about the cat who'd ruined Christmas.

"Hers was *so* rude," he told Birdgirl. The pigeon—who was working on an art project that involved a big pile of pinecones—looked up.

"Firsting of all, hers didn't even say hello or nicely to meet you!" he began, listing the insults on his left wingtip. "Nextly, hers brokened the decorations on the dead tree! And final, hers ruined the whole of Christmas."

Birdgirl gave a sympathetic coo, but it didn't make Megabat feel much better. He stared out the tiny shed window, hunched his wings up and grumbled as he imagined the wonderful Christmas going on inside the house without him.

Megabat was still mad the next morning when Daniel came out to get him.

"Priscilla won't eat her kibble, so Mom went to buy her some organic cat food in case she likes that better," Daniel said. "Mom'll be gone at least an hour. We can paint the steam engine now if you want."

Megabat had intended to tell Daniel to go play with his cat instead, since he seemed to like her soooo much, but at the sound of the words *steam engine*, his large ears perked up.

"Fine, fine," he said, coming to hang from Daniel's outstretched finger. "But only for a shortish time. Mine's gots a very busy day."

"Doing what?" Daniel looked around the shed.

"Helping Birdgirl with hers's project." The bat motioned toward Birdgirl's pinecones.

"What's she making?" Daniel asked.

In truth, Megabat hadn't bothered to ask yet, but when he flew over to give his beloved a good-bye peck on the cheek, he gasped in fright. Then he grinned. "Aha! Giant pretend puffer rats!"

Back when Megabat had lived on the papaya farm in Borneo, the farmer had put large dolls between the rows of fruit trees. The job of these saggy people was to scare away the birds—which was how Megabat knew what Birdgirl had in mind.

"Hers will be putting them in the yard," he said, showing the fearsome-looking decoys to Daniel. They were made from pinecones, rocks, acorns,

twigs and various things from the
recycling bin. Birdgirl was always crafty,
but this time she'd outdone herself.

"Theys will scare the real puffer rats away from stealing the seeds. Birdgirl! Yours is a genius."

"Coo-woo," Birdgirl said modestly.

Daniel, Megabat and Birdgirl worked together to move the scary pinecone statues into the yard. Then Daniel and Megabat went inside. Megabat was glad to see that Daniel had already brought the model steam engine and paints to the table. But instead of sitting down to start, his friend crouched near the buffet.

"Priscilla's been under here all morning," he explained. "Here kitty-kitty," Daniel called softly. The cat didn't emerge, so Daniel lay on his stomach to get a better look. "I guess she's still not too sure about us, but Mom says she'll probably come around in a day or two."

Megabat couldn't understand why Daniel liked the cat when she was no fun and all she ever did was hide. But he didn't want to get in trouble again, so he didn't say so. Instead, he got busy opening the little pots of paint. There were all the colors of the rainbow—plus a tiny pot of shimmering gold.

"Did you see how blue her eyes are?" Daniel commented, not getting up to help Megabat, even though the lid of the orange paint was stuck. Instead, he opened a bag of cat treats and shook one into his hand. "You don't get that with

just any cat. It's because she's so fancy
and purebred."

"Huh, how goes it?" Megabat
muttered. He turned the little pot
around looking for a pull-tab or
something, but Daniel mistook his
question for interest in the cat.

"It doesn't mean that she's *made of bread* or anything," he explained, holding out the treat. "*Purebred* means both her parents were the same breed of cat. Chocolate seal point Birmans. With beautiful markings on their faces and pure-white paws, just like hers."

Megabat abandoned the paint pot and shuffled to the edge of the table just in time to see the cat poke her nose out from beneath the buffet to smell the treat, then catch sight of Daniel and disappear again.

Megabat straightened his back and ruffled his wings importantly. "Interestingly, mine is being purebred also," he announced.

"No you're not!" Daniel laughed. That hurt Megabat's feelings.

"Mine is!" he insisted. "Both Megabats's parents was bats."

"Where's your certificate, then?" Daniel asked. "Priscilla came with a certificate from a breeder. Mrs. Cormier showed Mom. It has a gold seal on it and everything."

Megabat didn't have a certificate or a gold seal, or even know exactly what those things were. He gave a little huff and busied himself with the paint pots again. After getting orange open, he managed to do green, blue and purple without much trouble.

When he was done, he pushed the

steam engine into the center of the table and cleared his throat to let Daniel know it was time to begin.

"One sec, okay?" Daniel said over his shoulder. "I'm just going to open some canned tuna. Maybe that will get her out. Cats love tuna."

Daniel dropped the cat treat he'd been holding on the floor and left the rest of the bag on the table. He disappeared into the kitchen.

Megabat loved treats, so he teetered over and sounded out the words on the side of the bag. *F-ish Bit-ees*. He tilted the package, sniffed, then gagged.

The small brown lumps inside looked like beetle dung, but smelled worse. He couldn't imagine anyone wanting to eat one... but just then Priscilla's whiskers poked out, followed by her whole head. She glanced both ways to make sure no one was around. Then her nose began to dance as she crouched low and inched across the floor toward the treat Daniel had left behind.

When she reached it, she crunched the lump hungrily, and as she ate, Megabat studied her from above. Sure, the cat was soft, but she was kind of lumpy in places—especially around the back. And he couldn't understand the big deal about the markings Daniel had talked about. They were just brown smudges.

That was what gave him the idea.

Working quietly, so as to surprise Daniel, Megabat picked up a brush and dipped it into the pot of red paint. He made a big arc across his furry stomach, then added a swipe of orange, followed by purple, green and blue until a nighttime rainbow stood out brightly against his black fur. He definitely looked fancy now, but there was something missing.

Stars, of course. Nothing was fancier than stars!

Megabat dipped one talon and then the other into the little pot of gold paint and pressed them all over his wings to make sparkling patches. He added one

last star on his nose—the biggest, brightest of all.

"Ta-daaaaaah!" he sang, but Daniel was still in the kitchen.

"Just a sec," his friend called back. "Almost done."

Meanwhile, the startled cat froze on the spot. She looked up at Megabat. Her muscles tensed. Her eyes grew round and shiny as marbles.

"What does yours wanting?" Megabat asked. But, of course, the cat didn't give him a straight answer. She just kept staring.

Suddenly, it was obvious! Now that he was so beautifully decorated, the brown-splotched cat was sad that she wasn't the fanciest animal in the house anymore. Well, that was hardly his fault!

"Yes, yes." Megabat strutted to the other end of the table. "Megabat is gorgeous and yours is regular."

As if confirming how badly she wanted to be pretty like him, Priscilla looked up at the table and gave a soft, plaintive miew.

Megabat sighed. He couldn't help it. He felt a little bit bad for her. "Oka-hay, fine. Mine will giving yours *one* decoration."

He picked up the blue paint pot and went to drizzle a splotch onto her tail, but the cat dodged him. Perhaps she didn't understand that staying still was an important part of getting painted.

"Aha!" Megabat said. "Mine knows what will make yours stay non-moving." He held his breath against the stink, then pushed over the bag of cat treats that was sitting beside him. A big pile fell to the floor, and once the cat was hunched over eating, Megabat was able to get to work.

Mostly blue. Next purple. Finally, a few bright dashes of yellow. The colors made the cat look like the peacock he'd seen with Daniel at the zoo once—a huge improvement. But instead of thanking him, as soon as Priscilla had finished her fish bites, she began to turn in frantic circles.

"Stopping that!" Megabat shouted. "Yours will ruining the decorations before they dries!"

"What's going on?" Daniel came back into the room. "Megabat! Why is the cat blue?" He made a grab for Priscilla, but she dashed right past him toward the safety of the buffet, leaving paint marks behind on his pants.

"I prettied her while she eated stink bites," Megabat explained. "And looking! Ta-daaaaaah!" He stuck out his tummy and unfurled his wings to give Daniel the full night-sky effect.

But instead of marveling at the twinkliness of the stars, admiring the cheerfulness of the rainbow, and saying how gorgeous and clever Megabat was, Daniel gasped.

"Megabat!" he said. "What were you *thinking*?"

THE PLAN

When Daniel's mother got home from the store, she was *not* happy about the colorful cat or the empty treat bag.

"Daniel J. Misumi. Why *on earth* would you let Priscilla play in your paints?" She crossed her arms and pinched her lips. "And a whole bag of treats? She'll get sick to her stomach! Don't you have anything to say for

yourself?" But Daniel couldn't very well explain that a talking fruit bat had painted and fed the cat.

"No video games for the rest of the weekend," Daniel's mom said.

"But—" Daniel started. His mother silenced him with a look, then pulled a yowling, hissing Priscilla out from under the buffet, wrapped her in an old towel and went to run her a bath.

"Sheesh," Megabat said, once they'd heard Daniel's mother stomp up the last of the stairs. "Most cranky." But instead of agreeing, Daniel marched across the kitchen and threw open the back door.

"Out!" he said.

"But—" Megabat began. Daniel

copied his mother's pinched lips.

Well, two could play at that game. "Hmmph." Megabat crossed his star-covered wings over his rainbow tummy. "Mine was leaving anyway." Then he flew out without so much as a "seeing you later."

As he swooped across the yard, Megabat spotted Birdgirl pacing back and forth in the snow. "Yours will not be believing about that no-good trubble cat now," he announced as he landed beside her, but before he could properly launch into his tale of grave injustice, he noticed the devastated look on Birdgirl's face. She bobbed her head toward the largest of her squirrel decoys.

Megabat gasped. Attached to the closest statue's face, below its egg carton eyes and above its pine needle fangs, was a silly mustache made of dried grass. One of the smaller decoys had been knocked right over, and another wore a goofy pointed hat made of twigs.

There was a maniacal chattering in the trees above them. Megabat and Birdgirl looked up to see two puffer rats leaning over a branch. Their tails were twitching menacingly.

"Shoo!" Megabat yelled at the fat gray one. "Getting lost!" he said to the black one with the scraggly tail.

But instead of leaving, the squirrels stood up on their hind legs and tapped

their little paws together—a lot like how Daniel and his friend Talia high-fived each other when they passed a new level in their favorite video game.

"SKOOCH!" Megabat yelled. For such a small bat, he could have a surprisingly big voice. The squirrels retreated to a higher branch, but not before the gray one turned to waggle its bum at them rudely.

Birdgirl pulled the mustache off her decoy and pecked at the ground miserably. All the puffer rats had left behind were a few empty sunflower seed shells.

"Mine's sorry." Megabat wrapped one wing over Birdgirl to hug her, forgetting for a moment about his starry wings.

"Coo-woo?" Birdgirl asked when she noticed the sticky spots that had transferred to her own feathers.

"Oh yes! Ta-daaaaaah!" Megabat unfurled his magnificent wings to show her.

Birdgirl gave an appreciative coo-woo. She circled around him to get a better look.

"Thanking yours," Megabat said. At least *someone* liked his decorations. Daniel certainly didn't seem to like anything he did anymore. Not since that no-good, ruins-everything, hides-all-the-time cat had arrived.

He wished Daniel's family would just get rid of her… the same way they'd done a big clean-out that fall and gotten rid of the old blue cabinet that stuck out too far from the wall and the sewing machine that only worked sometimes.

Megabat had an idea! "Birdgirl! Coming here!"

"Coo-woo," she said, once he'd finished whispering in her ear. Suddenly, Megabat felt much better. With his brilliant plan and Birdgirl at his side, that cat would be gone in no time.

"And now," Megabat said, "about those rotten puffer rats..."

SO-NICE CAT
FOR SALE

The bat and the pigeon worked all
afternoon setting up their state-of-the-art
squirrel repellent system, but they had to
wait until the sun went down to put
Megabat's no-more-cat plan into action.

"In any minute," Megabat whispered.
The pair was perched on top of the
porch light. Almost on cue, the back door

opened and Daniel's father stepped out
holding a bag of garbage.

Megabat nudged Birdgirl and pointed
down with his foot. She understood

perfectly. With one smooth swipe of her wing, she pushed the snow off the top of the doorframe.

"Whaaaaa!?" Daniel's father shouted as the snow hit him in the back of the neck and slid down his bathrobe. He did a hopping dance, trying to shake it out. Here was their chance! Silent as shadows, Megabat and Birdgirl swooped through the open door and into the house.

Birdgirl—who wasn't usually allowed inside—followed Megabat through the kitchen, past the darkened dining room and into the living room. Megabat landed on the computer desk in the far corner. So far, so good. Only, when he looked around, Birdgirl was gone.

"Coo-woo!"

It took him a second to figure out why.

"Birdgirl!" he whispered. The pigeon had been distracted by the little shelf over the fireplace. Megabat couldn't exactly blame her. It was his favorite part of the living room too, especially since Daniel's mother had set it up to look like a tiny Christmas village, complete with fake snow and small houses that lit up from the inside. The village wasn't what had the pigeon's attention, though. She was busy looking at herself in the mirror over the mantel.

She tilted her head this way and that, as if trying to catch her own best angle, then pecked at her reflection and

preened her feathers before admiring
herself again.

There was no denying it: Birdgirl was
a pretty pigeon. But they didn't have
time for preening!

"La-la-la-la, pa-rump-a-pum-
pummm." Daniel's father had already

come back from garbage duty. He was walking through the house, singing and switching off lights. Any second now he'd pass through the living room on his way upstairs.

"Birdgirl!" Megabat whispered again.

At the sound of his voice, Priscilla, who'd been hiding underneath the big armchair, emerged. Megabat saw the cat's eyes lock onto the pigeon. She crept along, low to the ground. Her big, fluffy tail twitched this way and that. When she reached the floor near the mantelpiece, her back end began to wiggle in preparation for a pounce.

"Oh no. Don't yours dare!" Megabat said firmly. He'd seen cats hunt birds and squirrels in the yard before. He knew all too well what she had in mind.

"The drum-mer boy blah-blah," sang Daniel's dad, getting closer. "Pa-rump-a-pum-pummmm."

Megabat had no time to lose. He swooped onto the mantel to protect his beloved. "Birdgirl is not being a cat snack!" he muttered as he flew. He expected to land softly on the blanket of pretend snow, somewhere between the tiny library and the little post office, but he didn't know about the electrical wires hidden underneath. One of them caught in his foot as he came to a skidding stop, and the entire village shifted, as if it had been rocked by an earthquake.

Birdgirl took off into the air as miniature streetlights toppled, houses collided and a ceramic snowman went flying off the edge and shattered on the floor, right next to where Priscilla was sitting.

"Huh?" Daniel's dad said. His footsteps had stopped in the dining room.

"Hiding!" Megabat gasped.

Seconds later, Daniel's dad came into the living room and took in the scene: the broken snowman, the shaken village and the startled cat who was dashing back underneath the armchair. Fortunately, he completely missed Megabat, who had hopped into a small

wooden sleigh and borrowed a hat from a nearby Santa doll as a disguise.

"You!" Daniel's father said accusingly to the cat.

Daniel's mother ran down the stairs. "Oh no," she said. "What did she break now?"

"Your favorite snowman," he reported.

Daniel's mother reached under the chair and pulled out the cat. "Bad cat," she said, tapping Priscilla softly on the nose.

The cat, who was hanging miserably in Daniel's mother's arms, gave Megabat a bewildered look—no doubt disappointed there would be no pigeon treat that night.

"It's a good thing you're family now," she said. "I suppose we can forgive you *one more time*." Then, even though she was angry, she kissed the cat on the top of the head.

Megabat didn't dare move a muscle. In fact, he barely breathed for the long minutes it took Daniel's parents to clean up the broken snowman, turn off the lights and head upstairs carrying the cat.

"Huh," Megabat said indignantly, once they'd gone. "Nonefair! When Megabat breakings things, mine's sent to the cold shed. When hers gets in trubble, hers gets kissy-kisses."

There was a rustling in the branches of the Christmas tree as Birdgirl—who had concealed herself between two decorations shaped like peace doves— emerged.

"Coo-woo," she said, tilting her head, as if to remind Megabat that, actually, he'd been the one to break the snowman.

"Yours is missing the pointy." Megabat sighed. "It's *not* being about who brokened the snowman. It's being about nonefairness. Coming on. Let's be selling that no-good, bird-hunting cat." Megabat felt more certain than ever that it was the right thing to do.

The ingenious plan had come to him when he'd remembered how Daniel's mother had written a little story on the computer about the blue cabinet and the mostly broken sewing machine. Daniel had written one too, after he'd decided to sell his old bike. Megabat had helped.

They'd done it by using a special website for selling old stuff.

The very next day, a man with a van and a lady with a truck came and got the things. And, even better, they'd paid Daniel and his mother money before they took them away! Daniel had used his share to buy a brand-new Lego set for them to play with.

Writing their ad took all night—with Megabat sounding out the words and tapping the keyboard, and Birdgirl working the mouse—especially because they had to do a few drafts to get it just right.

Trubble Kat for Sael

Breakings things. Allweez hiding. No fun.

Mite eats yer bird.

$1.00

Birdgirl had shaken her head. Megabat sighed, but he knew she was right. When Daniel sold his bike, their story didn't talk about how the bell was rusty and the handlebars jiggled. Instead, they told about its bright red color and how fast it went. Things that were true, with the not-so-good parts left out. He erased the words and started over.

Trubble Kat for Sael
Meedium sized. Freshlee washed.
Eats stink treets. Tastes hairee.
$1.00

The new story was definitely better, but according to Birdgirl, it still wasn't good enough. Megabat grumbled as he hit Delete, but even he had to admit that the third story was sure to sell the cat— even if the last bit wasn't exactly true.

> Purdy Trubble Kat for Sael
> Fluffee. Fancee. Pure of bread.
> So nice.
> **$1.00**

Finally, just as the sun was coming up, they hit the Publish button. Then they waited by the door. When Daniel's mother went out for the morning paper, Megabat and Birdgirl made their escape and went back to roost in the shed after a job well done.

6

MRS. CORMIER

The next morning, Birdgirl and Megabat awoke to the familiar sounds of Daniel's mom tossing handfuls of birdseed onto the lawn and then closing the back door.

Megabat flew over to hang from the top of the shed window. "Birdgirl!" he called excitedly. "It's being time!"

Birdgirl swooped out of the shed and went to perch in the big tree. Megabat saw her land on an upper branch. They both watched the puffer rats dash toward the seed pile. The fat gray one rubbed its front paws together greedily while the scraggle-tailed black one started stuffing its cheeks. Three of their rat friends joined them as well.

Megabat signaled Birdgirl by tilting a shiny foil pie plate they'd found in the recycling bin. The squirrels were in the perfect position.

Megabat grabbed the string they'd threaded out the shed window, stretched across the yard and tied to the old birdhouse. Meanwhile, Birdgirl pushed the birdhouse. It took everything they had, but finally, between Megabat's

pulling and Birdgirl's pushing, the
birdhouse came loose, plummeting to
the ground below and landing—with
amazing precision—on the old horn from
Daniel's bike that they'd found in the
shed and buried in the snow.

HOOOOOOONK!

The sudden blast pierced the morning
air and the squirrels leapt three feet,
spun around and dashed up the fence as
if their tails were on fire.

Megabat flew out into the yard.
"Haha!" he cried. "Taking that, puffer
rats!"

Birdgirl came down from the tree and
together they collected the seeds and
brought them back to the shed for

safekeeping. It would be enough to keep Birdgirl fed for several days.

Now it was time to check if anyone had written back about buying the cat. But to do that, Megabat needed to get back into the house, which meant asking Daniel to forgive him for painting the cat. Luckily, Birdgirl's craftiness came in handy. She was busy with a new project—a sign for the door of their shed that would read HOME SWEET HOME. The *H*'s, *E*'s and *M*'s were made of dried grass, and the *S* was a piece of bent wire, but she was having trouble finding *O*'s. Still, Birdgirl selflessly put her own project aside and helped Megabat attach twigs to a piece of birch bark using tree sap as glue.

When it was done, Megabat flew up to Daniel's bedroom windowsill. He knocked twice with his wingtip, then pressed the bark up against the glass. It had taken them ages to sound it all out.

"Oh, all right, Megabat." Daniel opened the window. "You can come back in. Just promise you'll be nice to Priscilla."

Megabat crossed his wingtips behind his back and promised. Then he suggested going downstairs to work on the puzzle Daniel had gotten for Christmas. That way they'd be near the computer if it dinged with messages.

When they got to the living room, the friends examined the box and made a plan. The picture was of a park with a playground, a duck pond and a lady on a bench feeding pigeons. Daniel decided to work on the edges, while Megabat picked out the red bits that would make the playground's twirly slide. He'd barely finished his pile, though, when they were rudely interrupted.

"Priscilla!" Daniel laughed. The cat, who had finally stopped hiding, had jumped onto the coffee table. She was knocking around puzzle pieces with her paw.

"Stopping that!" Megabat said as the cat's fluffy tail swept some of his red pieces onto the floor.

"I think she's trying to help." Daniel smiled.

"Huh. Much unhelpful helping," Megabat muttered, picking up his pieces.

"No, really!" Daniel laughed. "She

found some matches. These three pieces make a pigeon!"

Megabat grumbled that they weren't working on the pigeon part yet.

"Miew!" Priscilla said sadly. She nudged the joined-up pieces toward Megabat with her paw and gave him an imploring look.

Was she trying to make a big deal over the fact that she'd found a match before him? He thought about telling her to stop showing off, but then he remembered he'd fake-promised Daniel he'd be nice to her.

"Hmm. Pigeons," he acknowledged gruffly. He pushed the pieces aside with his wingtip. "Mine will be working on thems next." Although, secretly, he probably wouldn't. He might even leave the pigeons till very last.

As they continued to work on the puzzle, Megabat kept a keen eye on the computer in the corner… but it didn't ding with a new message. Not once! Then, just as Daniel was fitting together the last edge piece to make the puzzle's frame, the doorbell rang.

Megabat's heart leapt. Perhaps it was someone coming to buy the no-good cat… but no. It was just Mrs. Cormier from three houses down. Had she come to take the cat back? Megabat waited, hoping…

The old lady was standing on the

hallway mat, stomping snow off her boots. Even from inside Daniel's pocket, Megabat could smell her perfume: like dead flowers coated in dust. It must have been tickling Daniel's nose too, because, right away, he sneezed.

"I hope I'm not disturbing you," Mrs. Cormier said. "But I can't stop wondering how Priscilla's getting on."

"Not at all!" Daniel's mother said. "Why don't you come in and have some tea and a visit?"

Mrs. Cormier took off her coat and walked into the living room. She smiled when she caught sight of Priscilla. "There's my princess," she said.

The old lady brushed some nearly

invisible lint off the sofa, then sat primly on the edge and patted her lap. Priscilla didn't hop up, so Mrs. Cormier reached down, grasped the cat roughly around the middle and pulled her onto her nylon-covered knee. "There's my precious angel buttercup." She kissed the cat with loud, smoochy lips. Priscilla wriggled and tried to jump down, but Mrs. Cormier's claw-like hand held her in place. The old lady stroked the cat's side and the corners of her mouth pulled down into a frown.

"Have you been brushing her?" she asked.

"Sometimes," Daniel answered. Suddenly, he sneezed so hard that

Megabat, who was hiding inside Daniel's pocket, had to grab on to the buttonhole to keep from falling out.

"Bless you," Mrs. Cormier said, but she didn't sound like she meant it. "Sometimes won't do," she went on. "Look at this." Mrs. Cormier pointed to a spot on Priscilla's back. "The fur's getting matted. She needs brushing. At least twice a day." Mrs. Cormier pulled at the knot in Priscilla's fur with her fingers. The cat flattened her ears and scowled.

Daniel's mother came in with a cup of tea for Mrs. Cormier, but the neighbor only took one sip before pronouncing it "lukewarm and much too strong." She set it down on the side table near the Christmas tree.

Ahhhh-choo!

Now it was Mrs. Cormier's turn to sneeze. "All right, Priscilla," she said to the cat, who was still wriggling on her lap. "You're getting me all furry. Off you go." She plopped the bewildered-looking cat onto the carpet.

Priscilla immediately dashed under the big armchair—and this time, Megabat didn't blame her for hiding. He'd hide too if Mrs. Cormier wanted to smooch him and pull his fur.

Mrs. Cormier picked the cat hairs off her skirt one by one and dropped them to the floor. And as she picked and dropped, she complained to Daniel's mother about uninteresting things—dry nasal passages, the cost of something called hydro, and how there were too many different types of yogurt these days.

Megabat was about to nod off to sleep when there was a loud rustling noise underneath the armchair. Mrs. Cormier got up to investigate.

"What on earth has Priscilla got there?" She bent over stiffly to look.

"It's probably just that foil ball she found the other day," Daniel's mother explained.

"Well, take it from her, would you?" Mrs. Cormier sounded impatient. "It

looks like a piece of trash!"

Daniel's mother sighed a little, but she got down on her hands and knees to retrieve it. Megabat peered out of the buttonhole of Daniel's shirt. He gasped! It wasn't *a piece of trash*! It was the head of Daniel's R2-D2. The special present he'd made Daniel for Christmas!

"She really seems to like it," Daniel's mother said, holding up the head.

Megabat didn't care if she liked it!

"Well, surely you have *more appropriate* toys for her," Mrs. Cormier said. Megabat couldn't have agreed more!

For a second, he almost liked the cranky old lady, but then she did the unthinkable! Mrs. Cormier took R2-D2's head from Daniel's mother and plopped it into her still-full teacup. "Be a dear and throw that out when you dump the tea," she said to Daniel's mom.

Through the buttonhole, Megabat could see the special present bobbing on the surface. He had to get it back! Without stopping to think, he launched himself out of Daniel's pocket toward the teacup, landing inside with a thunk and a splash. For a second, he sank to the bottom, but then he came up sputtering and grabbed onto the floating foil ball like it was a life preserver.

"Huh?" Daniel said, and the adults turned to look.

"Did one of your Christmas ornaments just fall into my tea?" Mrs. Cormier asked. She reached toward the cup to check, but luckily, Priscilla chose that moment to show off.

"Miew!" The cat hopped up onto the coffee table. "Miew!" She paraded back and forth through the puzzle pieces, swishing her tail grandly so no one would miss its fluffiness.

Mrs. Cormier sneezed. "Oh, you silly

thing! *Do* get down off the furniture."

But when she picked Priscilla up to drop her on the floor again, the old lady let out her biggest sneeze yet.

"There go my allergies," she said. "I need to leave." She started to fuss with her handbag.

Meanwhile, Daniel picked up the teacup before anyone else could get to it. "Shhhh!" he said to Megabat.

Suddenly, Daniel sneezed too. The cup rocked in his hands and Megabat had to wrap his wing over the side to avoid being washed out in a wave of tea.

"I hope you aren't allergic to cats too, young man," Mrs. Cormier said. Then she headed for the door with promises to stop by later with a proper catnip toy for Priscilla.

While Daniel's mother said good-bye, Daniel headed straight to the kitchen to rescue Megabat. "That was *way* too close," he said as he dried Megabat off on the bottom of his T-shirt. "Mom and Mrs. Cormier almost saw you!"

Daniel tucked the bat back into his pocket along with the foil ball just as his mother came into the kitchen with a weary sigh.

"Priscilla's *lucky* Mrs. Cormier's allergic," Daniel said. He dumped the tea and handed her the cup to put into the dishwasher. "Who'd want to live with a mean old lady like *her*?"

"*Daniel*," his mother scolded, but she didn't disagree.

"She smells like the air fresheners they use in gas station bathrooms," Daniel went on, wrinkling his nose.

At that, Daniel's mother gave him her *do not be rude young man* look.

"Well, it's true!" he said. "Her perfume kept making me sneeze."

Instead of scolding him again, this time Daniel's mother doled out a real punishment. "Get your coat," she said. "We're going to buy Christmas sweaters for next year's family photo."

"But *why*?! Christmas is more than three hundred and sixty days away."

Daniel's mother pointed out that the

sweaters would be on sale for exactly that reason. Then she went to get the car keys and Daniel's dad.

"Can you please, for once, keep out of trouble while I'm gone?" Daniel told Megabat before he left. "Just sit quietly and see how much puzzle you can get done, okay?"

Megabat promised he would be a very good bat, but, truthfully, he had no intention of working on the puzzle. He'd just come up with an even sneakier (and stinkier) plan to get rid of that no-good, always-hiding, pigeon-hunting, present-stealing cat, and this was the perfect chance to put it into action.

STINK POTION

As soon as Daniel and his parents left, Megabat got to work. He began in the kitchen, letting his nose lead the way.

"Perfects! So whiffy!" he said after he'd sniffed his way through the spices in the twirly rack and selected the smelliest ones. Next, he found a brown liquid with the aroma of fresh-baked cookies, some green soap that smelled like crisp, juicy

apples and a pineconey cleaner from
under the sink.

He mixed these together, then added

something called Moroccan mint extract. "For an exotic dash of *je ne sais pas*," he said grandly to himself.

Meanwhile, Priscilla sat in front of the glass doors that led from the kitchen to the backyard. She kept miewing and pawing at the glass, no doubt trying to distract him.

"Shush!" Megabat said as he worked the lid off a jar of pickles and poured the sweet-smelling liquid into his concoction. He had no time to waste. If he could cover Priscilla with stink potion before the family returned, Daniel was sure to start sneezing. The family would assume it was the trubble cat he was allergic to and, just like Mrs. Cormier had done, they'd give her to another unfortunate family.

Priscilla was pacing back and forth now, glaring over her shoulder at Megabat with each miew.

Megabat groaned. How was he supposed to concentrate with so much noise?

"Shushing up!" he said, but that only seemed to make her more determined. "What's yours so miewly about?" He flapped over to see. "Oh, peeze!" he said. The cat was watching the squirrels in the yard. "Those are just being the puffer rats." There was the fat gray one and the scraggle-tailed black one. Megabat noted with satisfaction that they weren't going anywhere near the seed place anymore. No doubt they'd been too frightened by the honking machine. Instead, they were on the opposite side of the yard.

"Theys is digging holes," he explained impatiently. "All theys ever does is digging holes. At least, when theirs isn't stealing all the birdseeds." But his explanation didn't do anything to soothe the cat. Instead, she seemed to get even more out of sorts. The fur on her back stood up.

Megabat ignored her and got back to work.

"Hmmmm..." he said, inhaling deeply as he stirred in each new

ingredient. Something green and gloopy
from a jar. A mysterious black powder. A
most delightful dash of colorful cake

sprinkles. The sun was just beginning to go down outside when he decided his concoction was nearly complete. He sniffed. It just needed a final ingredient. "Hmm, hmm, hmm," he sang to himself. He opened the upper cabinet.

"Aha!" His eyes landed on a big bottle of clearish yellow liquid. He sounded out the words on the label: "Fish *say-u-see*." He sniffed it and gagged. Megabat worked the cap off, then scooted around behind the bottle and pushed it hard. It tipped and the liquid glug-glugged out, splashing into the bowl and all over the counter and on parts of the floor.

When the bottle was empty, he flew down to the counter to stir again. Then he plucked a ladle from a jar on the counter with his talons, hovered above the bowl and scooped up a generous portion of goo.

"Coming here, kitty," he said. The cat was still transfixed by the puffer rats, which gave him the perfect opportunity. Megabat swooped crazily across the kitchen with his ladle and dumped the sticky potion onto her back.

When she leapt up and spun around, trying to see what it was, he took the opportunity to go back for a second spoonful. But by the time he reached her, the cat was hissing and backing into a corner with her ears flattened. For a second, Megabat thought he had her

trapped, but then the cat darted around him and ran out of the kitchen.

"Oh no. Yours isn't getting away so easy-peasy!" Megabat flew after her through the dining room, through the living room and into the front hall.

He would have caught up with her too, if it hadn't been for the fact that flying with the heavy ladle made him clumsy. Plus, at just that moment, there was a jingling of keys in the front door.

"We're home!" Daniel announced. His dad opened the door—but before the family could step inside, the cat flew past them and straight down the icy porch steps.

"Priscilla!" Daniel's mother dropped

her shopping bag full of Christmas sweaters and tried to grab the cat—but it was too late. The last thing Megabat saw before he hid behind a houseplant was the tip of a fluffy chocolate-brown tail disappearing out of sight.

LOST CAT

Megabat could hardly believe how easy it had been! Why hadn't he thought of chasing the cat out through the open door sooner? It would have saved a lot of trouble—not to mention mess.

While Daniel's parents went to look for Priscilla, Daniel stayed behind with Megabat.

Daniel sniffed as he walked into the

kitchen. "Ugh!" He picked up the bowl of stink potion and made a face. "Didn't I tell you to stay out of trouble? What were you doing in here?"

"Ummm..." Megabat stalled. "Making yours a most odorous snack."

Daniel dropped the empty bottle of fish sauce into the trash. "It's odorous, all right. And it's all over the place. Help me clean this up."

Daniel tossed Megabat a soaped-up sponge. The bat slid back and forth across the countertop on it, as if it were a skateboard. But Daniel wasn't having any fun. He kept walking over to stare out the back door.

"They should have found her by

now," he said with a sigh. "I mean, how far could she have gone?"

But many more minutes passed. The kitchen mess had long since been cleaned and darkness had fallen when the front door finally opened. Daniel put Megabat in his pocket and ran to find out what had happened. There was an icy blast of air as Daniel's parents closed the front door and kicked off their boots. Megabat peered out the buttonhole. They were *not* carrying a cat.

"Sorry, bud," Daniel's father said. "We searched the whole neighborhood."

"She's probably holed up somewhere warm… under someone's back deck, maybe," his mother added, rubbing her hands together to warm them. "I'm sure she'll be back first thing in the morning."

After that, Daniel's father made noodles and Daniel's mother set the table. There was even fruit cobbler for dessert, but Megabat was the only one who seemed to enjoy it.

The wind howled around the shed all
night. The next morning Megabat, who'd
been huddled under Birdgirl's wing for
warmth, was awoken by the sound of
footsteps crunching through ice. He flew
over to the little shed window and

scraped at a patch of frost. Birdgirl joined him and they both peered out.

There was Daniel, pacing back and forth. His breath was making little clouds in the air. He was clutching a bag of cat treats in his mittens.

With one wingtip, Birdgirl drew a heart shape on the frosted glass then added a jagged line down the middle. She looked at Megabat imploringly.

"Oh. Don't be being silly," Megabat said, rubbing out the broken heart. "Daniel will be forgetting the trubble cat soon."

But Megabat grew worried when, that day at lunch, Daniel's mother announced that they were having a party the next

night—and Daniel still didn't smile.

"Talia just got home from her grandparents' house. She and her parents are going to celebrate New Year's Eve with us," Daniel's mother explained. "Won't that be fun? We'll have pizza. You can even stay up until midnight."

As soon as she left to do laundry, Megabat blew into one of the honky noisemakers she'd brought up from the basement.

"Woooot! Party time!"

Daniel sighed, so Megabat ducked underneath a sparkly party hat. He scooted up the table, playing bumper cars with the other hats. "Mine's esscited for seeing Talia!" he said, leaping out from under the hat. "Isn't yours *esscited*, Daniel?"

"I guess," his friend answered dully. "It's just... I really wanted to introduce her to Priscilla. And now all I can say is that I had a cat, but I lost her."

Talia and her parents arrived just after dark the next night, carrying a stack of board games, a pillow-sized bag of cheese puffs and a large fruit platter.

"This is for Megabat," Talia whispered to Daniel, holding up the platter. At the sound of his name, the fruit bat poked his head out of Daniel's pocket.

"Oooooh!" He drooled at the sight of the melon chunks, grapes and fresh strawberries.

"I'm sorry about your cat, by the way," Talia said to Daniel as they headed for the TV room to start a game of Monopoly. "I've been keeping an eye out. I'm sure she'll turn up."

"Yeah. Maybe," Daniel said hopelessly.

"Where's your brother?" Daniel asked. Talia's younger brother, Jamie, wasn't Daniel's favorite person, but it seemed strange not to have him there.

"He's at a sleepover," Talia answered. "They're watching horror movies until midnight. Where's Birdgirl?" Talia asked in return.

"In the shed," Daniel answered. "You know she's not very good at keeping out of sight."

"Oh." Talia sounded disappointed.

Megabat—who'd been busy counting Monopoly money (and giving himself just a little extra)—glanced up in time to catch her looking out the back window.

"You know, though..." Talia said, "if we kept her in here, I bet your mom and dad wouldn't even notice. Not tonight." There was loud laughter from the dining room, followed by the clinking of glasses.

"And we'd have more fun. Birdgirl's always the life of the party."

This was true. Megabat had never met a pigeon who played Pin the Tail on the Donkey better.

"I dunno." Daniel glanced meaningfully at Megabat. "I've been in trouble enough lately."

"Okay," Talia said sadly. But then she added: "I guess I was just thinking, nobody should be alone on New Year's Eve. It's bad enough that your cat's out there by herself in the cold."

As soon as Talia said the words, tears sprang to Daniel's eyes.

"Sorry!" Talia bit her lip. "I shouldn't

have reminded you."

"It's okay." Daniel sniffed. "She's all I can think about anyway."

Talia smiled sadly, and then she went to the craft cupboard. A minute later, she was back with construction paper and markers. "How about if we just *try* inviting Birdgirl," she suggested as she laid out the supplies. "We can play music. Her dance moves always cheer you up. If she gets spotted, we'll just pretend she got in by accident."

When Talia kneeled down at the coffee table and started to write, Megabat abandoned the Monopoly money to watch.

Birdgirl: You are invited!
Please be our GUEST OF HONOR
for the New Year's Eve party.
Location: TV Room.
Time: Right now!

"Well..." Daniel said. "I guess it'd be okay."

"It'll be better than okay," Talia said cheerfully. "And she'll love getting this special invitation. That way she won't feel like we forgot her."

Daniel got out some red and gold glitter glue to add a fancy border, and when it was all done, he handed the card to Megabat. "We need you to do an important job," he said.

Megabat loved important jobs.

"Can you deliver this to Birdgirl?"

"Tell her we really, *really* want her to be our guest of honor," Talia added.

"Megabat will not delay!" He grabbed

the invitation in his talons and perched on the windowsill.

"Careful." Talia nudged the window open. "The glitter glue's still wet."

Outside, the wind was whistling, kicking up drifts of snow, but the sky was clear and the stars were bright. Megabat meant to head straight for the shed. He could hardly wait to see the look of delight on Birdgirl's face—only—WHOOSH! A gust of wind swept the card from his talons and blew it over the fence. "Oh no!" Megabat called, swooping after it.

He followed the card over the neighbor's back shed and nearly caught

up with it, but another gust carried it
sideways, out into the street.

"Coming back here."

The invitation kept floating, traveling

higher now, over the roofs of two houses, past the school and toward the busy street. It whizzed past the library and the coffee shop. Finally, the card came to rest in an alley beside the back entrance of a restaurant. Megabat recognized it from the sign as Burger Barn: one of Daniel's favorite places. He swooped down after the invite. "Aha!" he said. "Gots you!"

But before he could lift off again with the card in his talons, he heard an all-too-familiar hiss.

FOUND CAT

The cat was crouched in a cardboard box near a vent that was blasting meaty-smelling steam. Megabat couldn't even be sure at first that it *was* Priscilla. She wasn't very fluffy or clean. But then the hissing came again and the cat started to swish her tail—matted and dirty, but still thick as a feather duster.

"Oh," Megabat said, trying to act casual. "It's being yours."

The cat glared at him. She obviously hadn't forgotten about the stink potion.

In fact, Megabat could still see a sticky patch of it on her back.

"Well, mine's not the least bit happy to seeing yours either," he countered. He turned to go… but something stopped him. It was a greasy hamburger wrapper stuck to his talon. As soon as he'd shaken it loose, the cat lunged at it and started to lick it clean, glancing in his direction every so often to be sure he wasn't making any sudden moves to steal it.

When she was done, she turned tail, stalked back to the cardboard box and curled up inside.

"Well," Megabat said, trying to sound more certain than he felt. "Yours is seeming right at home here." After all,

the cat had a nice box... and judging by
the garbage that littered the ground, lots
of hamburger wrappers to lick. What's
more, she certainly didn't seem to want
his help. If he headed home now, Daniel
would never even need to know that he'd
found the cat. It would be for the best.

Megabat was just about to pick up
Birdgirl's invitation and head back to
deliver it when a man walked out the
back door of the restaurant with a trash
bag. Quickly, Megabat ducked
underneath the card to avoid being
spotted. The man kicked at the cat's
box. "You!" he said. Priscilla ran out. Her
feet scrambled against the ice and she
slipped, landing on her belly. The man

stomped and she managed to find her footing and dash behind the dumpster. "Mangy cat. I already told ya ta get lost," he grumbled before heading back inside.

Once Megabat's heart had stopped racing, a heavy feeling crept in. With the card still tented over him, he crept around the side of the dumpster.

"Is yours oka-hay?" the bat asked the cat. She was breathing fast and her fur was standing on end. In the big, dark alleyway, behind the dirty dumpster, she looked very small and all alone.

"Listening," Megabat went on, against his better judgment. "Perhaps yours should be coming home now."

The cat narrowed her eyes at him.

Instead of thanking him for his generous offer, she hissed again.

"Fine! Being like that!" Megabat turned to go, but the heavy feeling stopped him again. He remembered the tears in Daniel's eyes, and how Talia had said nobody should be alone on New Year's Eve. As much as he disliked the fancy cat, she didn't deserve to eat trash in an alley and be yelled at by a box-kicking man. Nobody did.

"Yours won't have to be eating garbage anymore," Megabat tried. "And Daniel's house is being nice and warm."

At that, the cat sauntered back to her box. Megabat had never met a prouder, more maddening animal! She thought she was sooooooo special, didn't she?

Suddenly, he knew *exactly* how to convince her.

Still carrying the party invitation like a tent over his head, Megabat followed the cat. "Fine," he said. "Staying here if yours wants. Just before mine goes, one question..."

The cat ignored him, but Megabat pressed on. "Daniel has asking-ed mine to invite yours to do a great honor... A very *important* job."

That got the cat's attention.

"Tonight is being New Year's Eve. And ours is having a party, seeing?"

He was about to hold up Birdgirl's invitation to show her, but he thought better of it at the last second. "*Scuzzi.*" Megabat turned his back on the cat and dipped one wingtip into the still-wet glitter glue that Daniel had used to decorate the border. He carefully covered the word *Birdgirl* with the word *KAT*. Then he cleared his throat and presented the invitation with a little bow.

"Looking." He pointed to the letters. "Yours is invited to be being our guest. New Year's is the fanciest night of the year. So ours is needing the fanciest guest."

The cat stared at him, unblinking.

"For fact," the bat went on, "this is saying kat will be being the *guest of honor.*"

The cat emerged slowly. She sniffed the card, and for a moment Megabat thought his plan had worked, but then she glared at the paper with distaste before swishing her tail and disappearing behind the dumpster.

Megabat shrugged his wings. He was just about to leave when the cat came back with something in her mouth. It took Megabat a second to recognize it as half of an onion ring—one of the foods Daniel always ordered when they came to Burger Barn.

"No, no," Megabat said. "Yours is disunderstanding. Mine was not asking yours for food. Mine was inviting yours to coming home for being a special guest."

The cat swatted the card out of Megabat's wingtips, then batted at it until it fell flat. She dropped the greasy onion ring on top and nudged it with her nose.

"Mine told yours!" Megabat said. "Mine is not wanting—" But then he noticed that the half-eaten, C-shaped onion ring had ended up right on top of his glittery *K*. "Is yours for sure?" he said. "*Kuh… Kuh…*" He made the *K* sound Daniel had taught him. "Kat is most definitely starting with *K*."

The cat nudged the onion ring again, and now that she mentioned it, Megabat wasn't so sure. Letters were sneaky. Sometimes *C did* try to fool you by making a *K* sound. Perhaps she was right?

And, even more surprisingly—he
realized with a shock—perhaps she could
read! Megabat couldn't help but look at
the cat with just a little bit of admiration.

"Oka-hay, fine then. Cat-with-a-C," he conceded, "will yours coming home?"

The cat tilted her head to one side, like she was waiting for a slightly better offer.

"Peeze?" he added reluctantly.

That did the trick.

SEEDS

Because the cat couldn't fly and her paws
were nearly frozen, it took them a long
time to get home. Priscilla picked her
way through snowdrifts and across icy
patches while Megabat flapped overhead,
urging her on and pointing the way. It
was blustering cold and pitch-black by
the time they arrived in Daniel's
backyard—but never had a guest of

honor been so warmly welcomed.

When Megabat knocked on the TV room window and told Daniel what had happened, Daniel ran to the kitchen, threw the back door open and scooped Priscilla up. "Mom! Dad!" he'd called joyfully. "The cat's back!"

The adults crowded around while Daniel's dad toweled the snow off the cat's fur and Daniel's mother opened a can of stinky cat food. Meanwhile, Daniel's eyes watered with happy tears, and Megabat, who was nestled in his friend's shirt pocket, licked them up while Daniel swatted at his tongue and laughed.

After that, Daniel's mother took the cat upstairs to give her a bath, and right before midnight, Megabat flew back to the shed to get Birdgirl. The pigeon was overjoyed to be included in the party, and, safely hidden from the adults in the TV room, she polished off all the cheese puffs left in the bowl. When Megabat and Birdgirl shared a beaky kiss at midnight, both of their faces came away sprinkled with beautiful orange dust.

It was a very good night indeed, but the next day things went back to how they'd been the week before—only worse. Instead of hiding, the cat slept on a special, soft pillow in the sunniest spot in the living room. She no longer played with R2-D2's head, but now she had all kinds of new toys. Dangly ones and jingly ones and ones that looked like little mice. Megabat wasn't allowed to play with any of them.

On top of that, even Daniel's dad admitted that the cat wasn't so much trouble after all, and the whole family made a bigger fuss than ever—brushing her fur, giving her treats, telling her "good job" when she pooped in a box and, most of all, trying to keep her from escaping again—until one day the next week…

"Mom bought this for Priscilla," Daniel explained. He showed Megabat a collar studded with twinkling diamonds. It was the most breathtaking thing Megabat had ever seen, and he burned with jealousy. "She won't stop scratching at the back door trying to get out," Daniel explained as he fastened the collar around Priscilla's neck. "Mom and Dad figure we might as well let her. I mean, she came back last time, right? With a little help." Daniel scratched the top of Megabat's head in thanks, which made him feel a little better—although he still couldn't take his eyes off that diamond cat necklace.

Priscilla, on the other hand, didn't seem to appreciate it one bit. She scratched at the collar with her back foot, but then she turned her attention to the door. "Miew!" she said insistently, looking back toward Megabat. "Miew!" Megabat followed the cat's gaze, but there was nothing in the yard except the puffer rats. And they were just doing what they always did: digging holes.

It hardly mattered. Since he and Birdgirl had devised their ingenious honking machine, Birdgirl had been safely collecting and storing the seeds in the shed. Let the rats dig if they wanted to.

"Miew!" the cat cried again. Daniel opened the door, and Priscilla leapt into the snow. But instead of going exploring, she made a beeline for the shed and began to scratch at *that* door.

"What does she want in there, I wonder?" Daniel said. "Come on... let's go see." He slid his boots on and tucked Megabat into his coat pocket.

"This is Megabat and Birdgirl's home," Daniel explained to the cat. "And we keep things like the lawn mower here too. See?" He threw the door open to show her.

But instead of the homey and well-ordered shed Birdgirl usually kept, the sight that met them was utter chaos. The rake was tipped over, the recycling was spilled everywhere and there, at the very back of the shed, was a terrified Birdgirl perched atop her pile of seeds, surrounded on all sides by chattering puffer rats.

Before Daniel or Megabat could react, the cat gave a low, menacing growl.

The greedy puffer rats were busy stuffing their cheeks with seeds as the cat crept toward them, her feather duster tail beating wildly. They hadn't seen her yet, but there was no missing her when, a moment later, she pounced and pinned a tail to the ground with her big furry paw. She hissed at a second puffer rat, baring her pointy fangs.

Megabat was used to seeing the puffer rats scurry here and there, but he'd never seen them move quite so fast. They jumped like bouncy balls. Three of them dashed straight out the shed door, but the last one—the fat gray squirrel— clung to the shed wall, frozen with fear.

Priscilla glared at the gray puffer rat and motioned with her head toward the corner of the shed. As if obeying her command, the gray squirrel—who was breathing hard and fast and making small squeaky sounds—inched down the wall and backed toward the corner.

"Daniel!" Megabat gasped. "Theys is thinking hers is the Queen Puffer Rat!" It made perfect sense, after all. She had the same puffy tail, but while the squirrels were small, silly and skittish, she was large, dignified and commanding—exactly like a queen.

A few seconds later, Megabat's theory was confirmed. The squirrel gave a humble little bow, as if begging her pardon, before disappearing into a small hole in the ground that Megabat had never seen before.

"Aha!" Megabat said. "Theys been tunneling in. Those rotten puffer rats has been trying to steal Birdgirl's seeds." And then he realized something else. "And the fancy cat has been trying to warn mine!" For days, she'd been staring out the back window, pawing at the glass.

The cat stepped toward Birdgirl, and
at first Megabat thought maybe she was
going to pounce on her too, but then

she swished her fluffy tail and miewed pleasantly, as if to say "hello," and maybe even, "nicely to officially meet you."

"Coo-woo," Birdgirl exclaimed, shaking her feathers in astonishment.

And then Megabat realized he'd probably gotten something else wrong! Maybe, when the cat had tried to hunt Birdgirl in the living room, she hadn't realized the pigeon was family! Perhaps that was why she'd pushed the puzzle pieces of pigeons together the next day—to apologize!

Sure, Priscilla had made some mistakes—like playing with R2-D2's head—and yes, she had hidden a lot at first... but maybe that was because she'd had to live all her life with mean old Mrs. Cormier. Perhaps all she really wanted was a home where she'd be treated with kindness and respect. And all this time, Megabat had tried to stop her from getting what every creature—fancy or regular—deserved.

Megabat flew out of Daniel's pocket and landed on the ground in front of the cat. "Mine's sorry," he said sheepishly. "Megabat should have been more nicer to yours and not tried to stink yours up with mine stink potion." The cat took a step closer and carefully licked the top of his head. It felt rough, like sandpaper, but Megabat didn't mind.

Then Priscilla turned, waving her

magnificent tail behind her, and went off to explore the shed.

"Is that why the kitchen was a mess that night and the cat smelled so bad when she came home?" Daniel said angrily. "Megabat! What did you think *that* was going to accomplish?"

Megabat hunched his wings up, feeling embarrassed.

"Yours didn't love Megabat so much anymore," he said in a soft voice. "Mine isn't fancy or fluffy." He held up one leathery wing, then let it drop. "Or pretty. Or pure of bread. Hers was stealing all yours's love away," he said with a little sniff, "like the puffer rats was stealing all Birdgirl's seeds. Mine

thought if hers wented away…" His
voice trailed off.

He half hoped Daniel would tell him
he was fancy too, but instead… "It's true,"
Daniel said flatly. "You aren't fancy or
fluffy or purebred." He paused and

Megabat felt his eyes start to well up with tears. "And love is *exactly* like seeds."

Daniel walked over and picked a seed off the top of Birdgirl's pile. Meanwhile, a single tear escaped from the corner of Megabat's eye and splashed to the floor. So the cat really had stolen Daniel's love, and now that Megabat had been a bad bat, he'd never get it back.

"Love is exactly like seeds," Daniel went on, "because it can grow."

Megabat blinked in confusion.

"Didn't you know that's what seeds do? They turn into new plants that make even more seeds."

"Yours gots a love plant?"

"No," Daniel said with a sigh. "What

I mean is, just because I love Priscilla too doesn't mean I love you any less, Megabat." Daniel went on. "It just means I've got more love to give now. You're *both* part of my family. And I love you the same amount, but in different ways. You're not fancy, but you're my best friend! Who else would watch *Star Wars* fifty times with me, or spin in the hammock chair till we puke? I'm always going to love you, okay? No matter what."

"No matter what?" Megabat asked.

"No matter what," Daniel answered.

By now, the cat was over in Birdgirl's craft corner, where the pigeon seemed to be showing off her work in progress: the HOME SWEET HOME sign for the shed door, which was still missing a few letters.

The cat walked around to admire it from all angles. She rubbed her face against it appreciatively. Or, at least, it seemed that way, but it soon became clear that she was actually scratching her neck… and she was getting pretty vigorous about it.

"What are you doing, Priscilla?" Daniel asked, walking over to see. "I hope she didn't catch fleas or something."

Birdgirl was the first to figure it out. "Coo-woo," she said, pointing to a spot on the sign with her beak. The cat had rubbed the beautiful diamond collar right off her neck and dropped it onto the sign where it made a perfect, glittering letter *O*. The most wonderful, wonderful gift from a cat who was much more wonderful than she'd at first seemed.

"Oooooh," said Megabat. "So niiiiice."

It really was a lovely moment.

Until they all heard the sound of footsteps out in the yard. "Daniel!" his mother called. "I just got the weirdest email from some guy who wants to buy our cat for one dollar! Do you know anything about an online ad?"

"Uh-oh." Megabat took off up into the rafters where Daniel wouldn't be able to catch him.

"Megabat?!" Daniel had his hands on his hips. "*Please* tell me you didn't try to *sell the cat.*"

"Mine didn't try to sell the cat," Megabat repeated obediently.

Daniel stared up into the darkness with disappointed eyes.

"Oka-hay, fine. Mine did *a little bit* try to sell the cat." Now Daniel looked really exasperated. "Don't forgetting yours loves mine *no matter what*!" Megabat reminded him.

And even though Daniel groaned and Priscilla's tail twitched in an oh-so-offended way, Megabat wasn't really worried. After all, they were family.

A Little Bit about Bats

Megabat is based on a real kind of fruit bat (or megabat) called the lesser short-nosed fruit bat. These bats are tiny, weighing between 21 and 32 grams—which is about as heavy as an AA battery, or a mouse—and live in South and Southeast Asia and Indonesia (Borneo), usually in rainforests, near gardens, near vegetation or on beaches.

Of course, even though Megabat is based on a real kind of bat, he's also made up. I don't need to tell you that actual bats can't talk... not even in the funny way that Megabat talks! But it might be worth mentioning that bats don't make good pets, either.

Bats are amazing creatures and an important part of our ecosystem. North-American bats eat insects, and they're rarely dangerous to humans. So if you see a bat in the wild, it's okay to observe it from a distance, but don't try to touch it or trap it!

Acknowledgments

It takes a lot of people to help a little bat shine. Big thanks to the warm and wonderful team at Tundra, especially the Sams (Sam Swenson and Samantha Devotta) for being Megabat's number one fans.

Huge gratitude to Kass Reich, who is not only lovely to work with, but who draws the cutest evil squirrels and the fluffiest fancy cats—and to Amy Jo Tompkins, agent extraordinaire, who finds each of my books the exact right home.

Finally, thank you to Cleo, for being the fanciest princess of a cat I have ever known, and to Brent, Grace and Elliot for being my people.